A CARIBBEAN COUNTING BOOK

ONE
WHITE
SAIL

Words by S.T. Garne
Pictures by Lisa Etre

GREEN TIGER PRESS
Published by Simon & Schuster
New York London Toronto Sydney Tokyo Singapore

GREEN TIGER PRESS
Simon & Schuster Building
Rockefeller Center
1230 Avenue of the Americas
New York, New York 10020
GREEN TIGER PRESS is an imprint of
Simon & Schuster.

Manufactured in Singapore

10 9 8 7 6 5 4 3 2

Library of Congress Cataloging-in-Publication Data
Garne, S. T. One white sail / by S. T. Garne ;
illustrated by Lisa Etre.   p.   cm.   Summary: A counting book
in rhyme describing the picturesque sights found
on an island beach.   [1. Counting.   2. Beaches—Fiction.
3. Islands—Fiction.   4. Stories in rhyme.]   I. Etre, Lisa, ill.
II.Title. PZ8.3.G1866On 1992 [E]—dc20 91-24662 CIP AC
ISBN 0-671-75579-X

For CL & KL and thanks ABD
—S.T.G.

To Kate with appreciation
—L.E.

One white sail
on a clear blue sea,

Two orange houses
and a slender palm tree,

Three girls walking
with baskets of bread,

Four boys skipping
on the trail to Ram's Head,

Five blue doors
in the baking hot sun,

Six wooden windows
let the cool wind run,

Seven old men
on a sparkling white beach,

Eight pink clouds
dancing just out of reach.

Nine steel drums
sing a soft sweet tune,

While ten boats sleep
'neath a pale island moon.

The illustrations for
ONE WHITE SAIL are
rendered in watercolor.
The text is set in
Avant Garde Extra Light.